Real Horse Art that YOU Co

Equestrian Parade

A Special Coloring Book for Horse Lovers

Ellen Sallas

Equestrian Parade
All Rights Reserved
Copyright © 2015 Ellen Sallas

ISBN-13: 978-0615984261
ISBN-10: 0615984266

Little Roni Publishers / Byhalia, MS
www.littleronipublishers.com
@LittleRoniPublishers

This book may not be reproduced, transmitted, or stored in whole or in part by any means, including graphic, electronic, or mechanical without the express written consent of the publisher except in the case of brief quotations embodied in critical articles and reviews.

Illustrations may be colored, cut out, and displayed without legal repercussions. Ellen C Maze, aka Ellen Sallas, holds the copyright –as well as the only right to profit financially –to each image indefinitely.

100% of the Illustrations within are originals of Ellen C. Maze, aka Ellen Sallas.

PRINTED IN THE UNITED STATES OF AMERICA

A Note from the Artist

I think I was born part-horse, because my earliest conscious thoughts were regarding the equine species. As soon as I could manage a crayon, I was drawing them. A horseless child, I sought every possible opportunity to ride or pet horses and ponies that crossed my path: the pastures around my small town of Millbrook, AL, trail horses when on family vacation, and the recalcitrant mounts of my summer camp exposure, all served to fulfill my horse-fix until I became a freshman at Huntingdon College in Montgomery, AL. There, I signed up for a Jan-Term of "Horsemanship." For two weeks, we learned to ride English and how to care for a horse. ELLEN WAS HOOKED. I soon bought a green Appaloosa/QH (Lil' Top Amber) for $700. I proceeded to ride and train her in 3-Day Eventing for nearly 15 years, until her retirement in 2004.

Ellen and Amber competing at J3 in Mississippi, 1999

This coloring book is for horse-and-art-loving children as well as adults who simply enjoy looking at horses. There's something about the horse in art – the soul of the equestrian goes into every painting. I suggest removing the art you're working on with a X-acto blade or sharp scissor, and then use color pencils, crayons, or even markers, to make this art your own. If you use color pencil, the shadows will show through (as on the cover example) and give you a more finished look for framing and display.

Go have fun!

SUGGESTION: Use crayon, pencil, or graphite for best results on this type of paper, and remove pages carefully with an Xacto Knife. ☺

Ellen Sallas

For legal purposes, I own the copyright to profit from this art, but you can certainly color it and display it to your heart's content. I removed my signature on most of them for your enjoyment, but copyright remains by US Law.

Ellen and Amber at Foxwood Farms Eventing Barn in Pike Road, AL, 1998

ALSO FROM LITTLE RONI PUBLISHERS
Check out these super-fun books for kids!
www.littleronipublishers.com

Vlad the Inhaler, Lorraine Mace, Illustrated by Ellen Sallas
Vlad has it tough. His parents are missing and his evil relatives are trying to kill him to steal his inheritance. Adventure, peril, and a few new friends make this tale the talk of 2014.
Middle-Grade, boys and girls, 9 and up
$9.00/$3.99 Paperback/Kindle
ISBN: 978-0615946528
Coming April 2, 2014 from Little Roni Publishers

Curse of Yama, KF Ridley
C. Walker Adventures, Book Two
When Dad unleashes upon himself a deadly curse, its up to 12-year-old Chloe to come to the rescue. Decode the map, find the seed, and defeat Yama...Yeah Right!
Middle-Grade, boys and girls, 9 and up
$7.50/$.99 Paperback/Kindle
ISBN:978-1467968911

A is for Apple: A Horsey Alphabet,
Ellen C. Maze and Elizabeth E. Little
Twenty-six fantastically limber horses bend and twist into each letter of the alphabet.
Humorous Illustrated Alphabet book
$9.50/$.99 Paperback/Kindle.
ISBN: 978-0615719450

In Pursuit of Sir Unicorn, by Ellen C. Maze and Elizabeth Little
While out on a trail ride on a lovely summer's day, the man and his horse meet a giant unicorn. The adventures that ensue take the man over hill and dale in pursuit of the most elusive of mythical creatures. Will he get his horse back from the unicorn? Read along in rhyming prose and find out!
Rhyming Fantasy Tale, Read-Aloud or Early Reader
$12/$2.99 Paperback/Kindle
ISBN: 978-0615778273

Let's begin with Dressage.

Turn on the Forehand

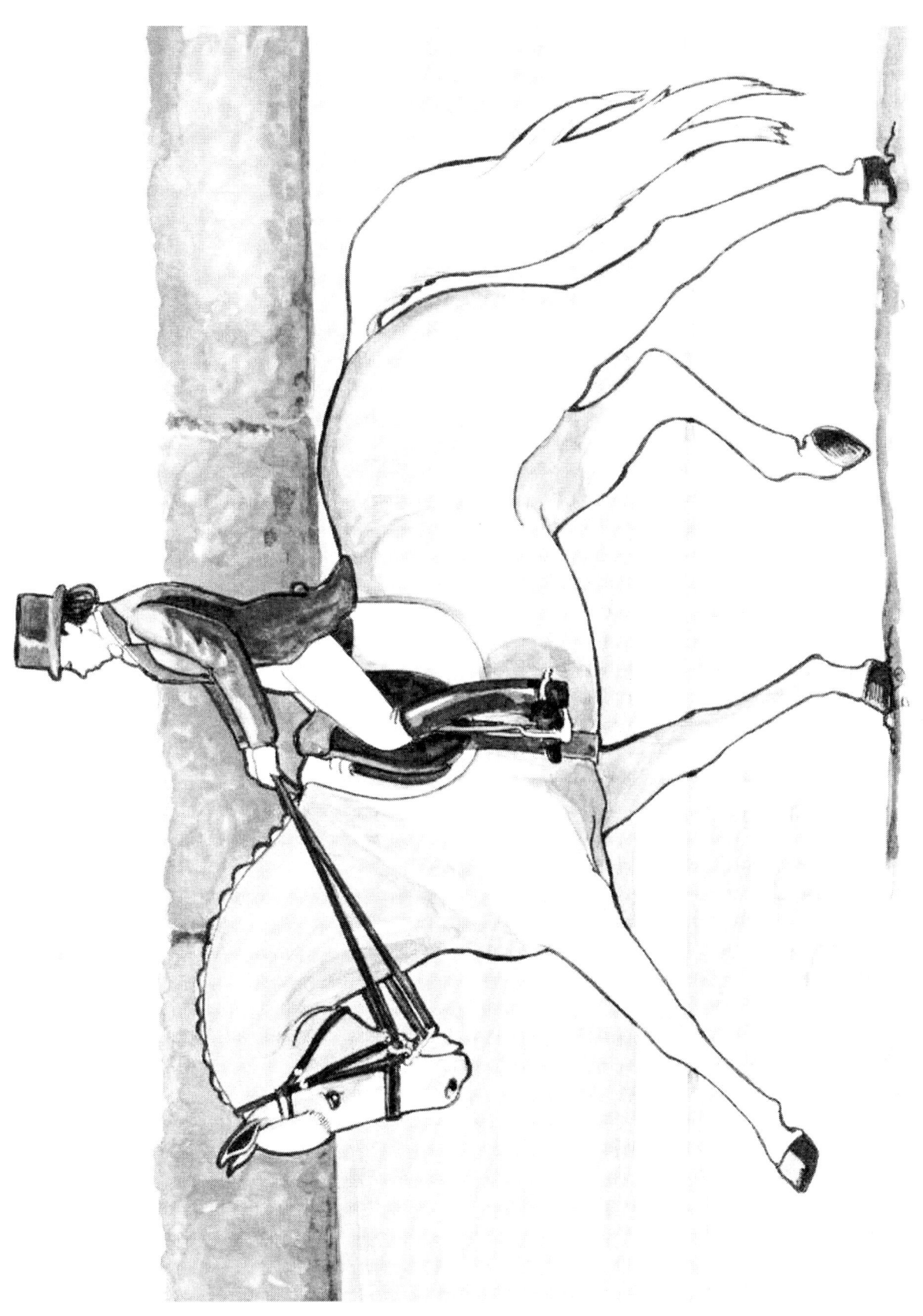

Extended Trot

Dance Dance Dance

Halt Salute

Learning Extended Trot

Olympic Galliard with Denise Rath

Junior's Novice Dressage Test

Pirouette Pro

Pirouette Pro 2

It's time to hop into

CROSS-COUNTRY JUMPING!

AKA XC

AKA Eventing...

Paint into Water

Coffin Easy

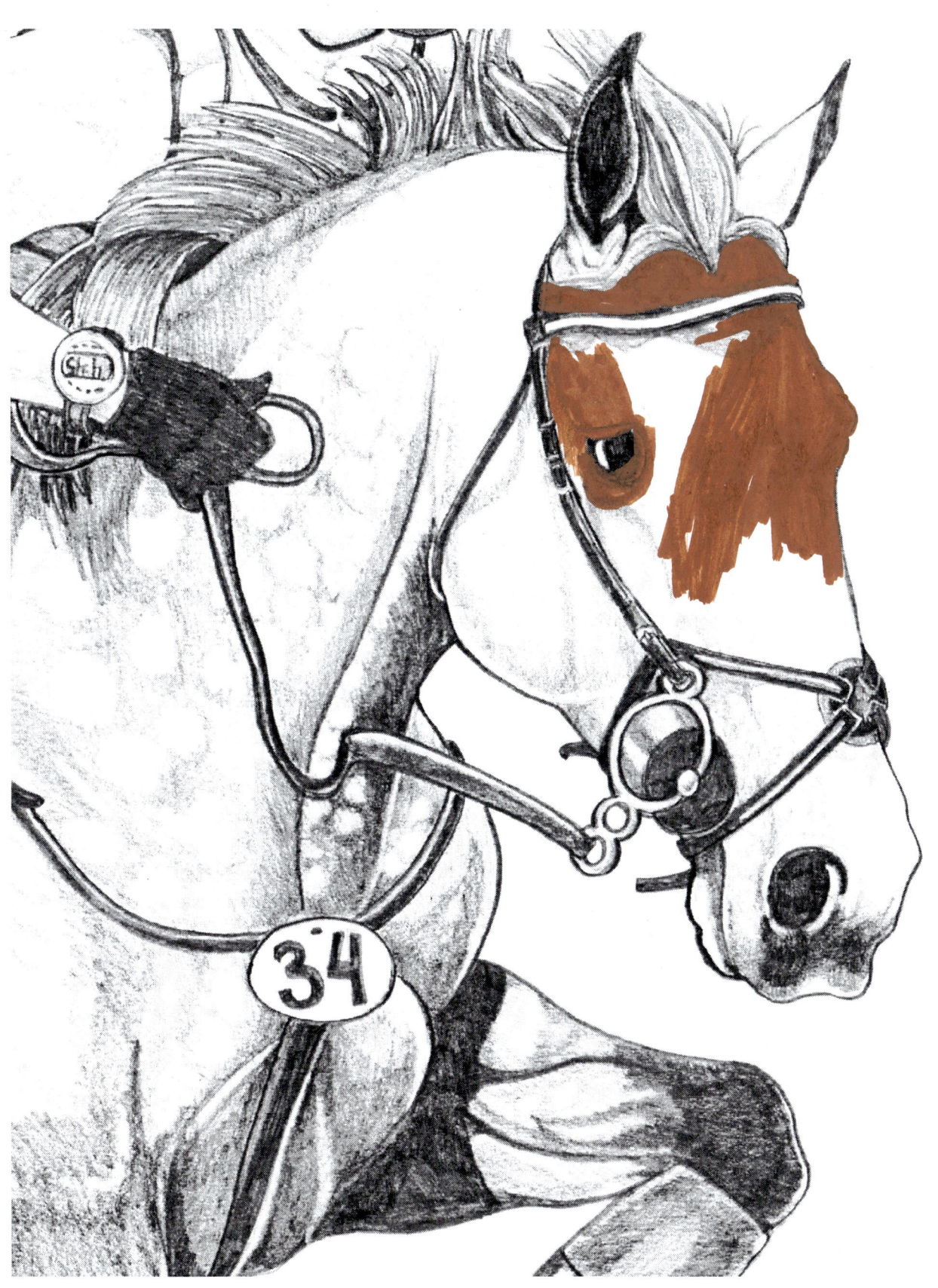

Climbing Over

The Exuberance of Youth - Start Box

Flying Paint

Into the Woods

Half-halt at the Water

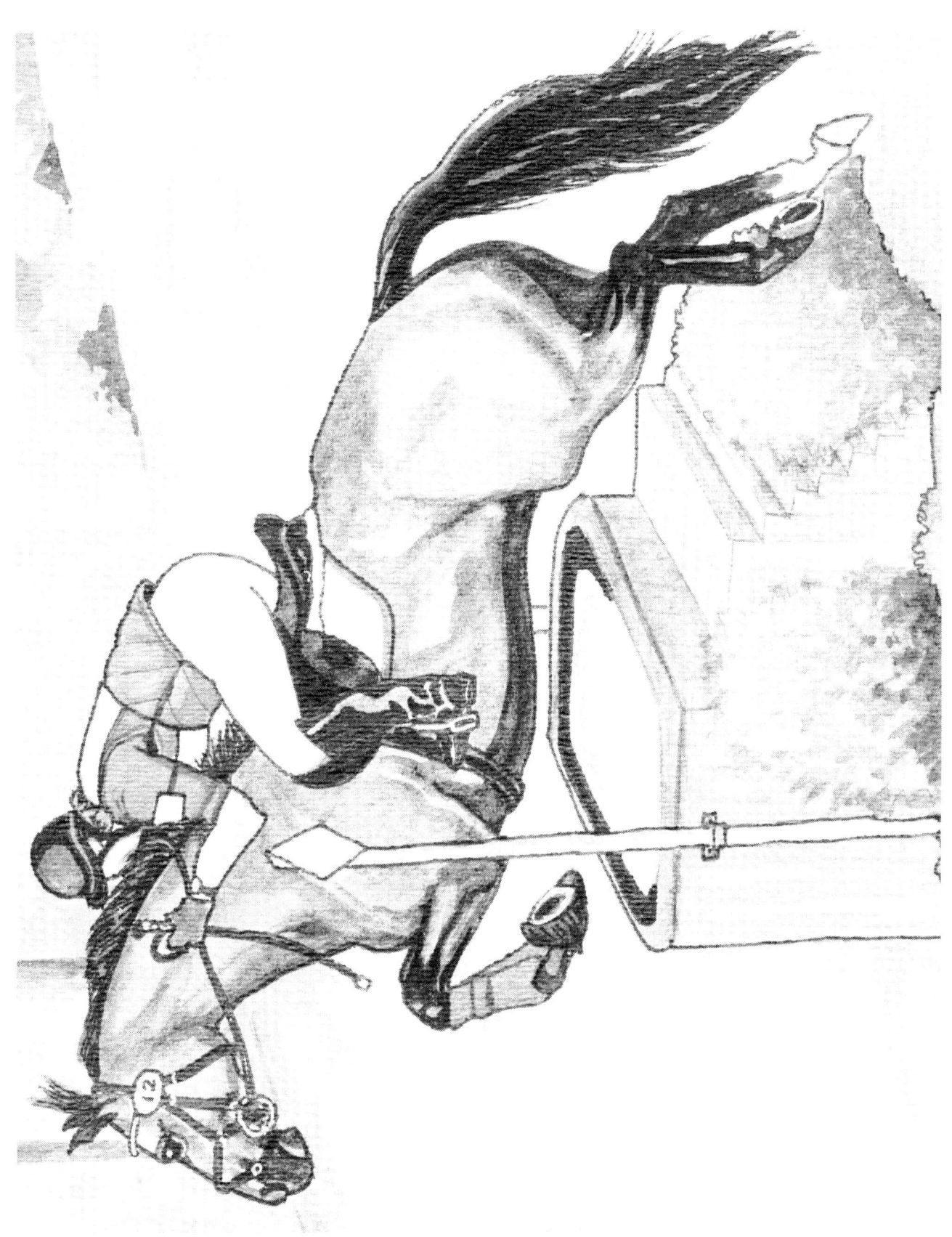

Jumping Jacuzzi

Into the Deep

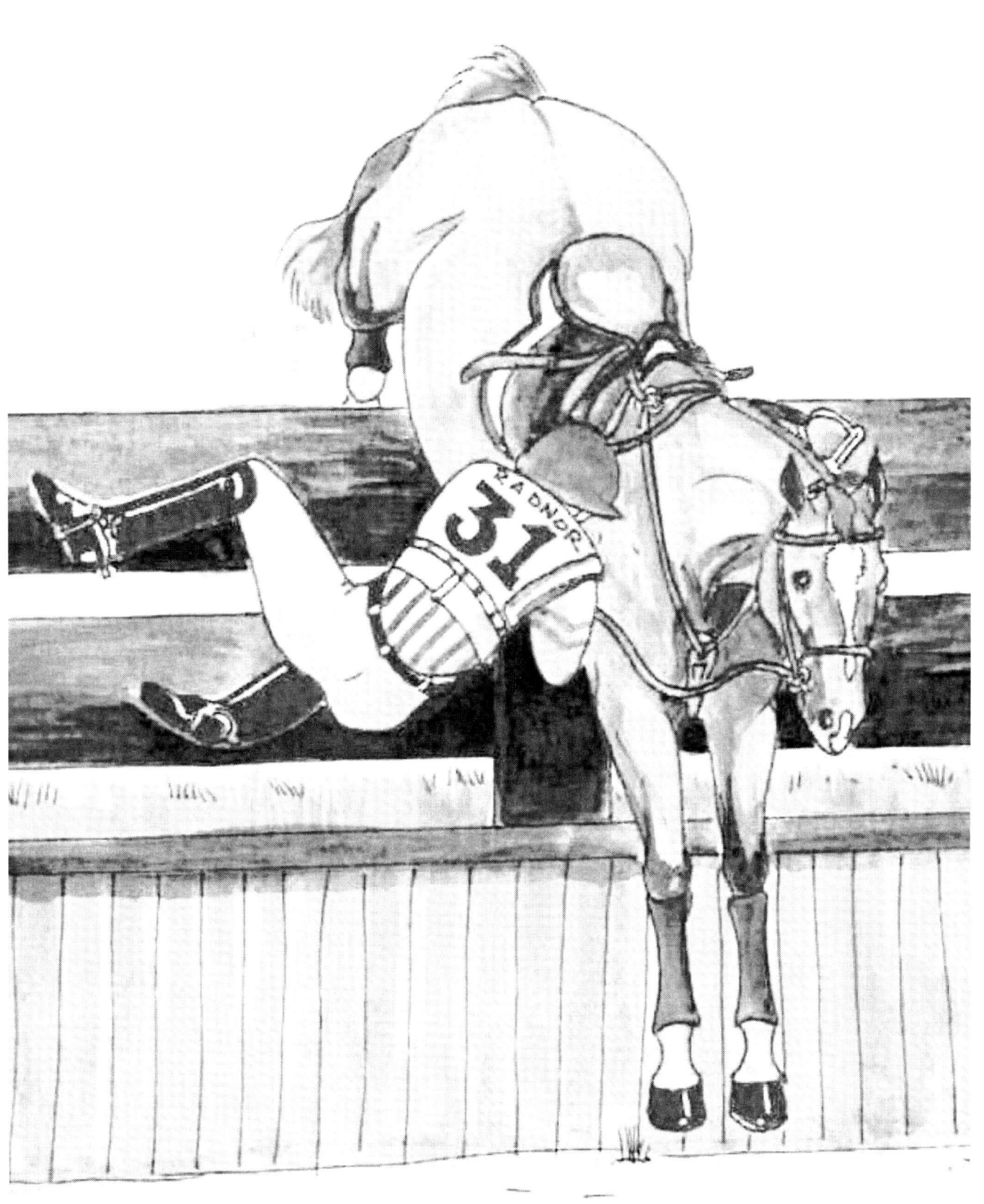

Going for a Swim

Going for a Swim Part 2

Paint Out of Water

Making the Time

The Turn in the Water

Paint Horse Dressage

Pony Power BN Log

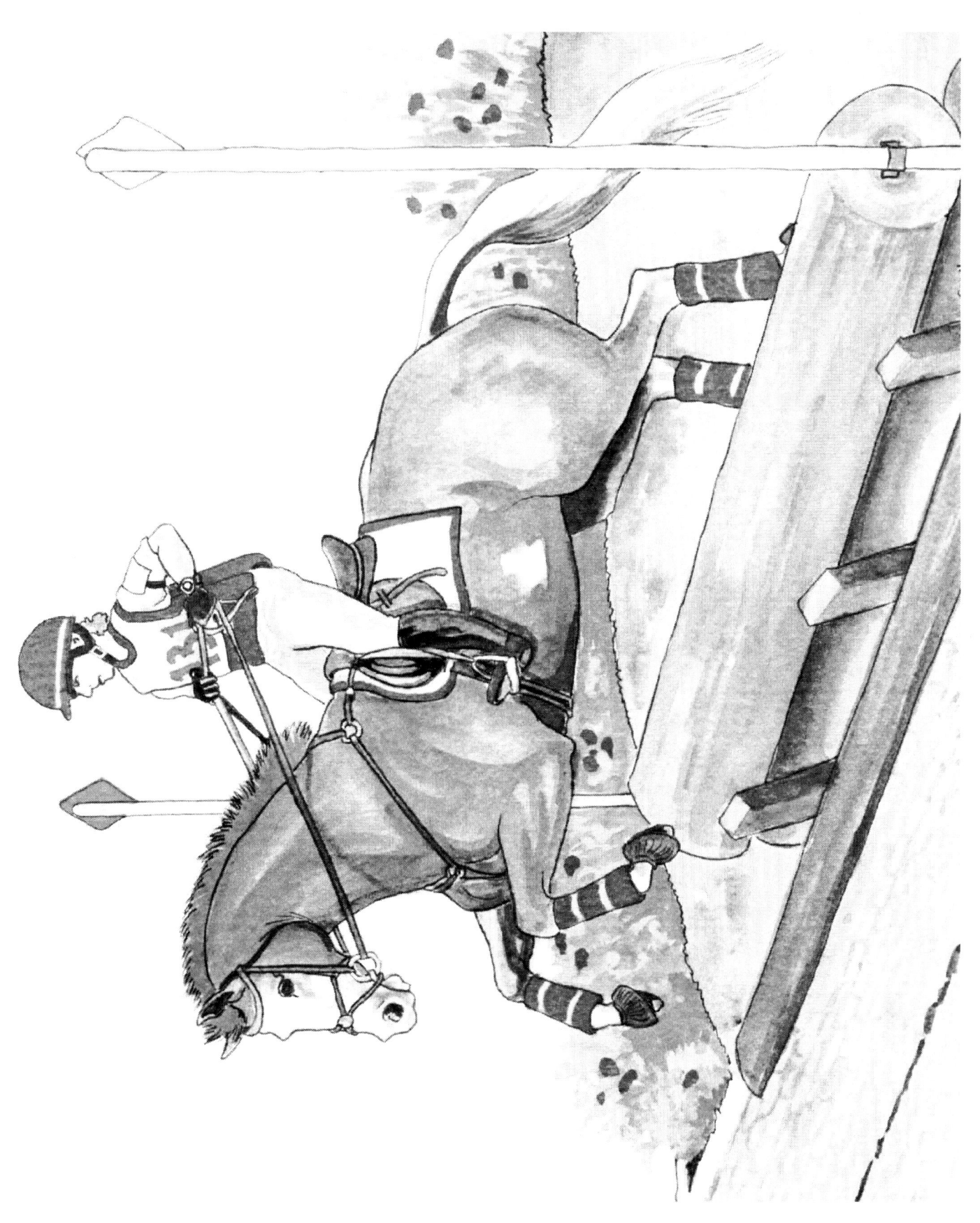

Water Log Water

Hang On Harry

Spotty Lad

Landing Nailed

Long Spot Water Exit

Water Lip

Table by the Lake

Flying Solo

Good Boy!

Log Off, Take Off

No Peeking!

Belgian Draft X/C

Water Corner

Ditch Handicap

Paint the Bank

Finally, getting classy with

Showjumping

AKA **Stadium**

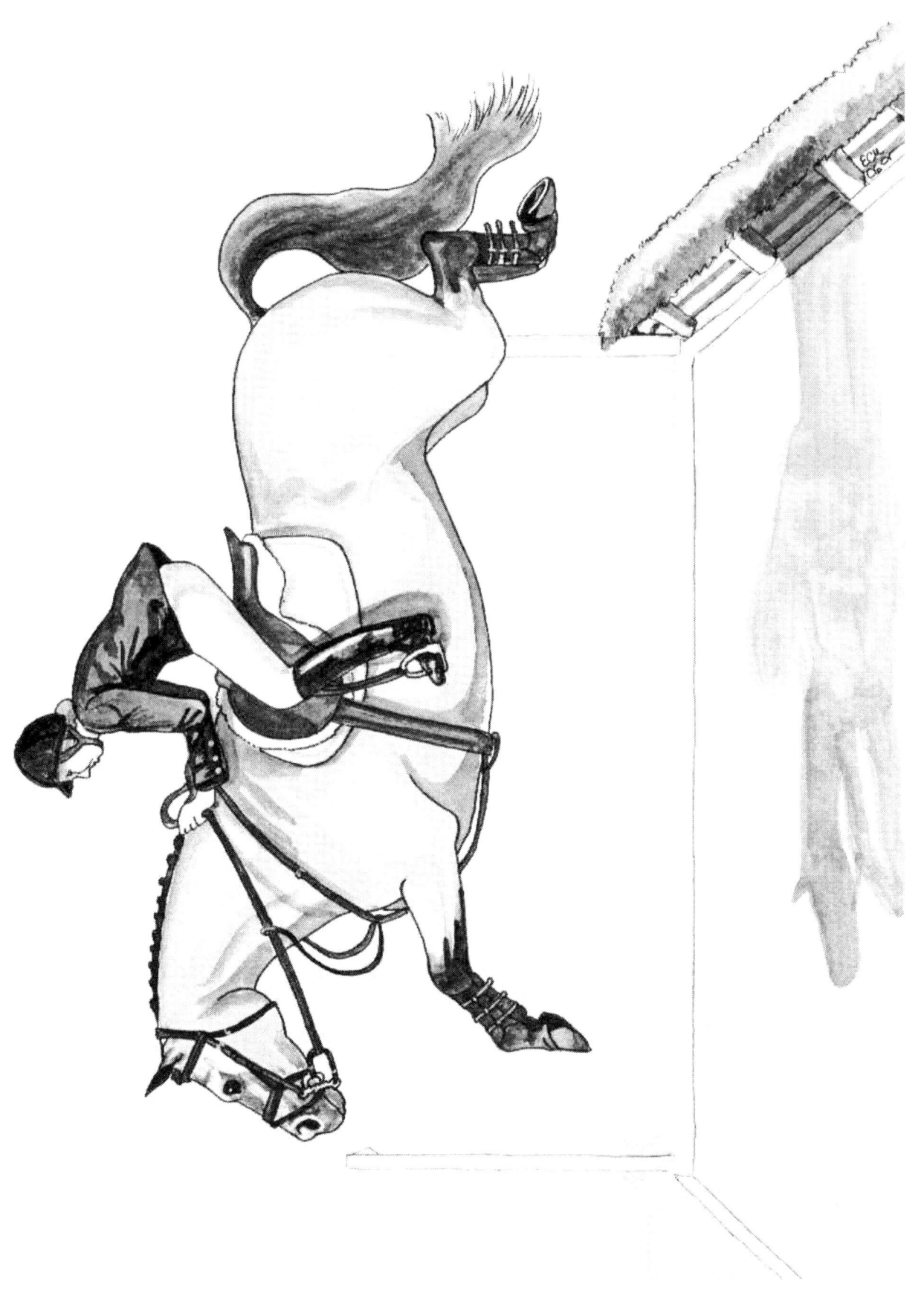

London Liverpool

A Star over Stripes

Caution: Brakes Without Warning

Scary Circus Jump

Maximum Effort

Derby Bank

Flying Grey

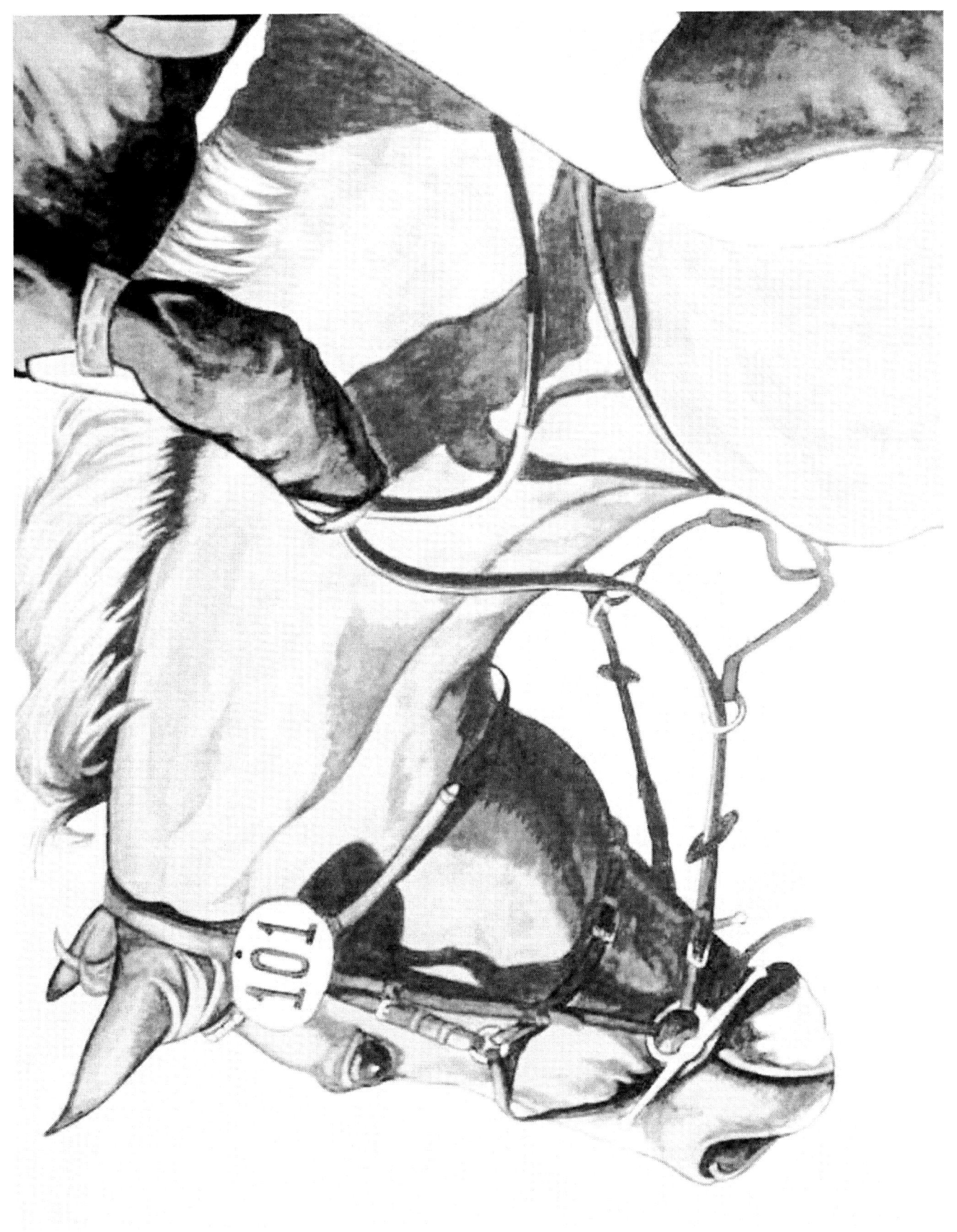

#101

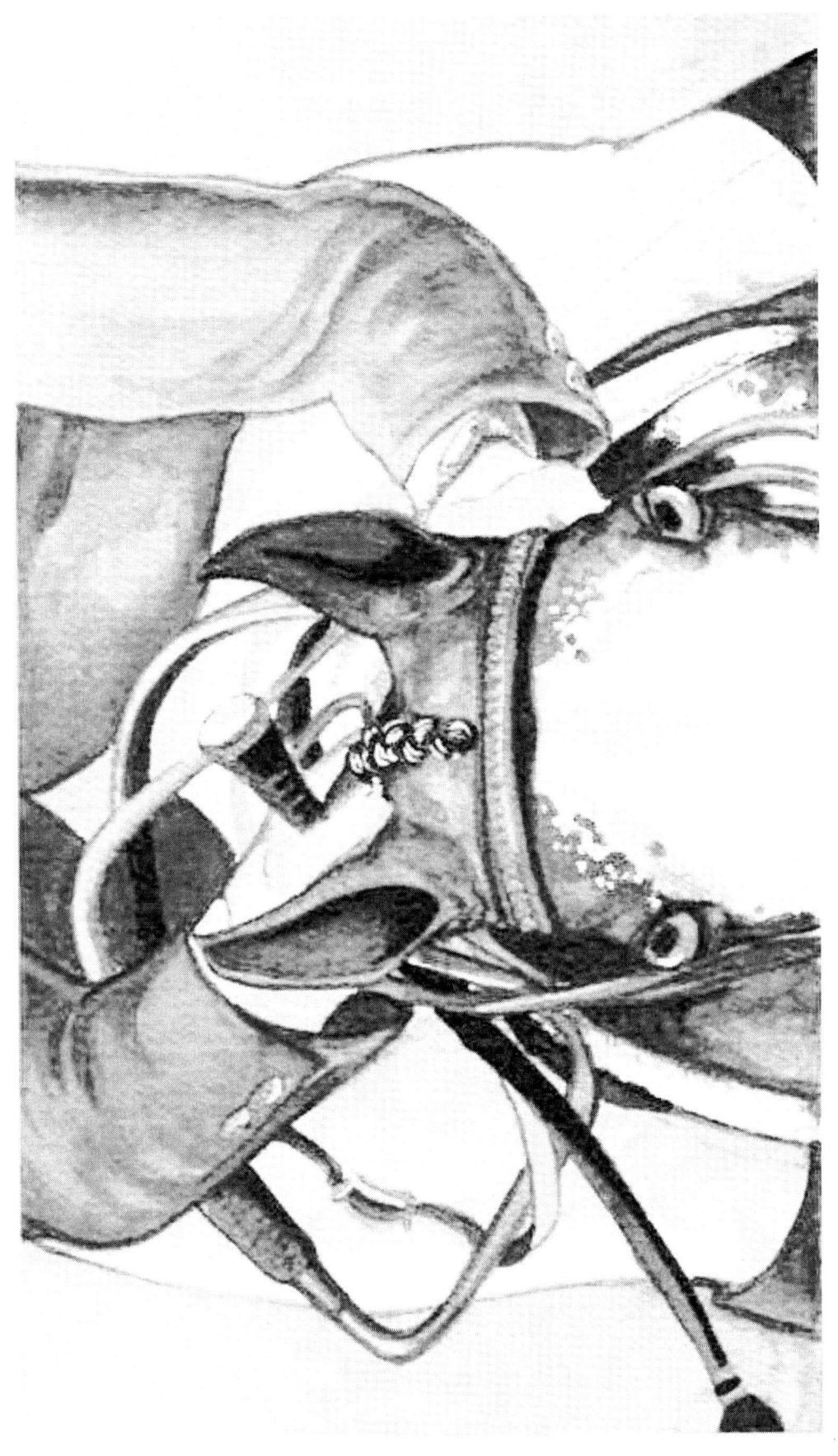

Ol Blue Eyes

Oops Rail Down

Stadium Elegance

Partnership

QH Champion Mare

About the Artist

Bestselling author and artist Ellen Sallas has been drawing horses even before she could walk. An avid horse lover herself, Ellen has been known to ride horses over hill and dale while daydreaming about stories yet written.

Ellen lives with her husband and vivid imagination in North Alabama.

Ellen has sold her art worldwide as an acclaimed animal portraitist for nearly 30 years. You can purchase much of this art as prints made from the originals at https://www.etsy.com/shop/giddyupstudio or by email, ellenmaze@aol.com.

Contact:

https://www.facebook.com/ellen.maze

https://twitter.com/ellenmaze

www.ellencmaze.com